D1438019

995189186 1

Published in 2021 by Mortimer Children's Books Limited
An imprint of the Welbeck Publishing Group
20 Mortimer Street, London W1T 3JW
Text and illustration © Welbeck Publishing Limited,
part of Welbeck Publishing Group
ISBN: 978 1 83935 121 1

This book is not endorsed by Epic Games, Inc. All images of Fortnite
characters/gameplay © Epic Games, Inc.

Writer: Eddie Robson
Illustrator: Oscar Herrero
Designer: Melinda Penn
Design Manager: Matt Drew
Editorial Manager: Joff Brown
Production: Rachel Burgess

A catalogue record for this book is available from the British Library.

Printed in the UK
10 9 8 7 6 5 4 3 2 1

All game information correct as of September 2021

Disclaimer: This is a book of fan-fiction and all characters, names,
gameplay described in the book are fictious and imaginative for
entertainment purposes and general information only and should not
be relied upon revealing or recommending any specific direct secrets
and methods of the game. The Publisher and the Author are not
associated with any names, characters, trademarks, gameplay, service
marks and trade names referred to herein, which are the property of
their respective owners and such use in this book is purely coincidental
and/or for identification purposes only. This book is a publication
of Welbeck Children's Limited and has not been licensed, approved,
sponsored, supported, endorsed or has any association with Epic
Games Inc and any of the creators of the Fortnite video game.

SECRETS OF A FORTNITE FAN

LLAMA DRAMA

EDDIE ROBSON

CHAPTER 1

I'm sneaking around, trying to put off the big confrontation as long as I can.

I know it's only a matter of time, but hopefully I'll get a chance to catch them off guard and they won't know what's hit them.

I can't wait any longer, I'm going in...

I walk into my house and find Mum and Dad both in the kitchen, chatting.

I drop my school bag in the corner and say, really casually: "Hi Mum, hi Dad, hope you had a nice day, mine was great, can one of you lend me your debit card please?"

They stop chatting.

Neither of them says: "Of course, Tyler, we're sure you'll use it responsibly so we're not even going to ask what it's for." Which is disappointing.

"Why?" says Dad.

"No," says Mum.

Well, it was worth a try.

"I just need to buy some V-bucks for Fortnite," I say. "It won't cost very much. I'll pay you back, or you can take it out of my pocket money, whatever's easiest."

"Why can't you just buy the things with money? Why do you have to buy these 'bucks'?"

"Because that's just how it works," I say.

"I don't understand it."

"You don't have to understand it, you just have to buy them for me."

"Haven't you spent enough on it already?"

"I've never spent any money on it, ever."

Mum looks at me suspiciously.

Mum thinks I'm an idiot.

"It is free to play," says Dad. "I checked it out."

"Why do you need to spend money on it now?" says Mum. "Is it one of those things where there's a free trial and then it costs loads to keep going?"

"No, nothing like that," I say. "I just want to buy some stuff to make the game more... fun."

This is sort of true - I think it will make the game more fun.

But the real reason I need to do it is because Ellie said I had to.

And of course, if I told Mum that she'd say "Well, if Ellie told you to jump off a cliff, would you do it?"

As it happens I have jumped off a cliff because Ellie told me to - in Fortnite, that is.

Her reboot card was at the bottom of the cliff and it was just about to time out, and there wasn't time to go round the long way.

(I didn't survive.)

Anyway, I have to do what Ellie says because she's the leader of our squad.

In two weeks' time we're entering a local tournament called Llamafest and I won't be allowed on the squad if I'm still using the noob skin.

(I dunno who they'll replace me with, because everyone else we know who's any good - Amy, Jake, Leon - is already in a squad.)

Ellie reminded me of all this today during lunch break at school, when we had a strategy meeting in the playground - just her and me and Sana.

Alfie, the fourth member of our squad (and, weirdly, Ellie's boyfriend) wasn't there, because he goes to a different school.

ALFIE

A new season has just launched, so we needed to talk over what's changed and make sure we all know our way around the new map.

Ellie was in a bad mood anyway because her favourite weapon has been vaulted and one of her favourite locations has suddenly become really popular.

When I told her I hadn't done anything about getting a new skin yet, she rolled her eyes. "You're really letting the squad down, Tyler."

"Sorry," I said, "I was just -"

"He's been waiting for the new season so he can buy the Battle Pass," said Sana.

"Haven't you got the new Battle Pass yet?" said a voice belonging to someone behind me, as if it was the dumbest, most hilarious thing in the world.

I turned around and there was Leon. He's a friend of ours, *supposedly*.

"So what?" said Sana.

"I'm already at level 37," Leon said, grinning in that annoying way he does.

No you're not! I was spectating your match last night and you're only on 19!

Ah, that was yesterday. I'm at 37 now.

"Shut up, it's impossible to get that far up the levels that quickly." A lot of things wind Ellie up, but nothing more than Leon lying about his Fortnite exploits.

Of course, Leon knows this and so he makes this stuff up just to annoy her.

"Are you losers entering Llamafest then?" Leon said.

"No, actually," I said, "because we're not losers." This sounded better in my head.

"You're not entering then?"

"Obviously we're entering," said Sana. "Tyler just meant -'

"Are you playing with that weird kid who doesn't do eliminations?"

"Shut up and go away," said Ellie, screwing her eyes up. Leon doesn't know Alfie's her boyfriend, and she doesn't want him to.

"So you've got Weird Kid," said Leon, "Noob Skin Boy -" he pointed at me as he said this - "and Anger Management Girl," he said, pointing at Ellie. "Sana, you can come over to my squad any time."

"I told you last time," said Sana, "and the five times before that - no thanks."

Leon shrugged and walked away. Afterwards Sana and I left Ellie to seethe on her own for a bit.

"Don't worry," she said, "I'll take you through how to set up the Battle Pass."

"Thanks," I said, "but that's not what I'm worried about. My parents are bound to make a big deal about me spending money on Fortnite."

"Why?"

"Because they like making a big deal about things."

Just then, Maisie walked past and said, "I knew it!"

We looked around. "Knew what?" said Sana.

"I knew you two would get together!"

We both laughed, a bit loudly and a bit weirdly. "We're not... no, we just..."

Then the bell rang to signal the end of lunch and we dashed inside...

Anyway, back to now. As I predicted, Mum and Dad are making a big deal about it.

Mum thinks it's silly to spend money on something that only exists in a game. But Dad says at least if it exists in a game it's not yet another thing I can leave in the middle of the living-room floor.

"Well, it's your money," says Mum and goes back to her laptop.

Dad pays for the V-bucks and I buy the Battle Pass.

I've got a bunch of messages from Sana guiding me through the Battle Pass - which I showed Mum and Dad to convince them it was a good idea, because they think Sana's more sensible than me.

I mean, they're not wrong.

> So there are lots of cool skins and other stuff you can buy in exchange for V-bucks, but for about half the price you can buy a Battle Pass.

> There's a new Battle Pass for each season, and it means as you go up the XP levels you can earn rewards... skins, wraps, accessories, music and loading screens.

> You'll have already picked up a few things if you've played through earlier seasons without the pass, because some of the items are free to all players.

> When you buy a Battle Pass you get one new skin straight away, and if you play through the whole Battle Pass up to level 100, you'll get about five new skins... with matching gliders, wraps, harvesting tools and back bling!

Even if you only play enough to unlock 30 or 40 levels... which is pretty easy to do... you'll end up with plenty of new stuff.

So it's a much better deal than just buying one new outfit from the store, even though there are some really cool ones!

If you want to be really smart with your money, there's a way to earn enough V-bucks to buy the next Battle Pass without having to buy any more...

Often you can earn 100 V-bucks as a reward for levelling up. You can spend these... or you can save them!

On previous seasons I've reached the end of the Battle Pass and earned more than enough V-bucks to pay for the next one! You just have to have the willpower not to spend them on other stuff...

Hope that's enough info for now. Sana x

After playing for a while with the Battle Pass activated, the game does feel different.

When you get rewards for going up the levels, the game feels more... well, rewarding.

It gives you a different way to get satisfaction out of playing the game, beyond getting eliminations and victories!

It also makes you focus more on ways to earn XP - because the normal ways of playing the game don't actually earn you that much! Not even a Victory Royale.

There are other ways of racking up that XP - and many of them have nothing to do with fighting other players...

CHAPTER 2

Suddenly I feel really motivated to go up a few levels - my favourite skin in the Battle Pass unlocks at level 50, and I'd like to get it in time for the tournament.

I don't really care what Ellie thinks, as long as she gets off my back... but I worry Sana thinks I don't look cool enough?

Er, in the game, I mean.

So I launch into a match - let's get that XP up!

"So what's the difference between the weapons then?" asks Dad.

After Dad helped me buy my V-bucks, I'd expected him to wander off. But he's still there - sitting on the sofa watching me play.

"Er," I say as I thank the bus driver, "just different ranges, and they do different damage, and different rates of firing. They're just different."

"Yeah, but which is which?"

"Well, range sort of goes pistol, then shotgun, SMG -"

"SMG?"

"Submachine gun, Dad. Then assault rifle, and then stuff like bows and sniper rifles."

"So what's the best one?"

"Well different ones are good for different situations, that's the point."

"Why are you going over there? Isn't it better to land in the middle and keep out of the storm?"

"Not necessarily - everyone goes to the middle so it's harder to grab a weapon and you can get plunged straight into a fight before you're ready."

"Oh."

I land and start bashing through a roof.

"Why are you doing that?" asks Dad. "Why not just land on the ground and walk in the door?"

"Because higher ground is safer, so if someone attacks you, you're in a better position - and there's often stuff in the attic you can't get to any other way."

I immediately demonstrate this by finding a random shotgun, an ammo crate and a chest.

"You know what I don't get?" says Dad, just when I thought he was going to stop asking me questions.

"Everything?"

Hang on... I'm sure I just heard someone moving around...

"What's the point of building?"

"It gives you cover, and you can reach higher places, and being higher is always an advantage in combat."

"But if you build a whacking great tower, everyone will know you're there, won't they?"

"Yeah, that's why the best players learn to build really quickly. That way they can build it at the last moment, when they're already getting shot at."

"Can you do that?"

"No, I can't."

"Why not?"

"Because I'm not good enough at building to -"

I knew it! Someone's shot me!

Annoyingly, night has fallen in the game (why does it have to do that?) so I can't see who's shooting at me or where they're shooting at me from!

I panic, wheeling around and firing randomly –

But it's no good. When you get to the point of wheeling around and firing randomly you're already dead.

"What went wrong there then?" asks Dad.

"Someone kept asking me questions."

Dad holds up his hands. "I'm just interested."

"Why, though?"

"Because you're interested in it and I'm interested in what you're doing. Is that not allowed?"

"Not if you're getting in the way of me actually doing it."

"Fine," he says, stands up and leaves the room.

I have no idea what that was about.

Dad's confusion over which weapon is which seemed silly to me, because I play all the time... but even people who've played the game forget the basics. I sometimes come up against players who are just obviously using the wrong weapon for the situation - like a shotgun at medium range.

Always make sure you've got the weapons you need in your inventory, and use them at the right times!

And certainly don't use explosives at close range - they're the only weapons you can damage yourself and your teammates with!

I'm always coming across rooms that have obviously been searched - there'll be an open door or an open chest in the corner - but they haven't been searched thoroughly.

OK, sometimes you're in a hurry and sometimes you want to get out and do something more exciting.

But pros always search the room!

A lot of players don't bother with food boxes, for instance - but these are always worth opening.

Sure, normal food items aren't as good as medkits and bandages, so they're usually not worth carrying - I just eat them if I need them, otherwise I leave them behind.

But shield mushrooms are ALWAYS good to find, because they top up your shield beyond the point where small shield potions stop working!

And though they give less shield than a regular potion, they're really quick to eat - so if you can stack them up, they can be useful for a quick top-up in the middle of a fight.

Search ceilings and hidden rooms too - chests are often hidden in places like this.

Elevators with closed doors often have something behind them.

And check bathtubs and toilet cubicles - it's easy to miss ammo crates and weapons hidden in these, because you don't have the light and sound made by chests.

The biggest thing is ALWAYS OPEN AMMO BOXES!

It's wild how many unopened ammo boxes you see around the map - often in really obvious places.

Always open them, unless all your ammo is full and you can't carry any more!

There's no such thing as having "enough" ammo - the ideal situation to be in is having so much ammo you never need to think about running out.

The quickest way to build up a big stock of ammo is to take it from other people - again, it's surprising how many people don't pick up loot from eliminated players.

Sure, stopping for dropped loot can be risky, and it's the moment when you're most vulnerable to long-range attacks, so sometimes you have to leave it and move on.

But it can be done very quickly - don't look down at the ammo, just run over it while looking out for possible attacks, and don't stop moving.

Throw up some walls around the dropped loot if you have to because that extra ammo can make a huge difference when it gets to the endgame!

The last thing you want to be doing is checking your ammo stocks, or switching to a weapon that's not the best one for the situation because your assault rifle just ran out of ammo.

Speaking of ammo - always reload, all the time!

It's so easy to forget when there's a lot going on - even if you think you've already reloaded, there's never any harm in twitching that reload button again.

If your weapon is already loaded, you'll just get a message telling you this – or that you don't have enough ammo to reload, which is also good to know.

The only downside of reloading is other players can hear you doing it, so it can be a problem when you're hiding.

But this just shows why you should do it regularly! If you already reloaded on the way, you won't need to reload when you get to safety.

Get into the habit of reloading when you're running from place to place.

It slows you down very slightly, so don't do it if you're running from the storm or there are opponents around – but when you're already running, the sound of reloading will make no difference.

I often come up against people who just seem to be shooting wildly around... almost as if they're not aiming properly?

Just a guess, but these people don't seem to be using the aim trigger.

You may as well shoot with your eyes closed!

Aiming brings up your crosshairs and, more importantly, it changes how you move around.

It slows down the movement of the camera and your character - both of these help you to find the target.

Once you start using the crosshairs in this way, it becomes second nature!

CHAPTER 3

Next day at school I'm eating lunch with my friend Jake.

"Technically I'm not meant to be talking to you," I say. This is because he's on Leon's squad. "Ellie thinks Leon will get you to spy on me and work out our strategy for the tournament."

"And," says Jake, "Leon said be careful in case Ellie's told you to give me a load of fake information about your strategy to throw us off."

"Yeah," I reply, "Ellie told me to do that if I did end up talking to you."

"Are you going to?"

"I considered it, but in the end I decided it was just too complicated."

"Agreed. Like, we could just talk about something that's not Fortnite, couldn't we?"

"Yeah."

We think for a minute about what that could be.

I'm just about to suggest talking about Minecraft when something hits the floor just next to our table.

I look down and see Amy sprawled there.

Now, Amy's tough. You could say she was the toughest girl in school, but she'd probably fight you for suggesting some of the boys might be tougher than her.

Amy and me are sort of friends though, after we did a design project a few months ago and I discovered she's super cracked at Fortnite.

She stopped barging into me on purpose in P.E., anyway.

A bunch of boys on the next table are sniggering, and it's obvious they tripped Amy just now.

This isn't going to be pretty to watch...

But to my amazement, Amy just gets up and walks away, without even turning to look at the boys.

"What just happened?" I ask Jake.

"Amy's dad told her she can't enter Llamafest if she gets into any trouble at school," he says. "At all."

Wow. So people are taking advantage while they can, I suppose.

But I'm not sure I'd like to be in their shoes when Llamafest is over...

Later, as I'm on my way out of school, I pass the same gang of boys shouting and jeering – something about a gorilla having escaped from its cage?

For a moment I think they're shouting at me – but no, they're shouting at Amy, who's walking up just behind me.

She strides past me and then past them too,

pretending they're not there.

They run out of jokes about Amy's appearance and start on her intelligence instead.

"Amy's so dumb," one of the boys says, "she's the only person who could throw a rock at the ground and miss!"

"Her name used to be Mary, but she couldn't spell it so they changed it!"

Amy's almost out of the door when she turns and looks at the boys with absolute fury in her eyes.

"Oooh," they say, pretending to be scared - or maybe they're pretending to be pretending to be scared, because I think some of them suddenly aren't sure if this was sensible...

Amy starts walking towards them. "You are going to regret that so much - all of you."

She starts pulling her arm back, getting ready to punch the nearest one -

"Stop!" I shout, and dash over, putting myself between Amy's fist and the boys.

It does occur to me at this point how stupid this is, but it's too late, I've done it now.

"You don't want to do this!" I tell Amy, who looks very puzzled. "Llamafest! You don't want to miss it - these losers aren't worth it."

One of the boys starts moaning about me calling him a loser, then he seems to realise I'm the only one stopping Amy from pounding him at the moment, and he shuts up.

Amy bites her lip, and I remember how she hates being told what to do.

Then she turns and walks out of the school, and the boys start laughing again.

"She's not stupid, you know," I say to them as I follow Amy outside.

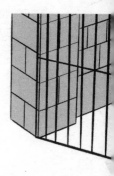

"Amy!" I shout, running to catch up with her.

"Go away, Tyler."

"I just thought you'd regret it if –"

"Do you know how embarrassing that was?"

"Well... yes, but –"

"If you do that again, I'll beat them up and use you as a weapon."

Then she storms off, and I wait for her to get a good distance away before I start walking.

Well, that was a waste of time.

But it did remind me of something... picking your battles is a very important part of Fortnite!

You can't really tell how good a player is by just looking at them.

You could assume someone in a noob skin isn't brilliant... but some people just don't spend money on the game, or might have got locked out of their account and made a new one.

Likewise, you could assume someone wearing the hardest-to-unlock skin on a Battle Pass is really good... but they might have just paid for some level boosts.

So the only way you can really know is to watch how they play - and that's not easy to do either!

Be careful of anyone who's really good at building - they're the hardest players to fight. Wait and see if someone else takes them out for you.

Sniper battles are hard to win, because you have to stay still to line up your shot - and if the other player is ready to fire, they'll get their shot in first. So take cover and try to draw them in closer.

And don't run around buildings looking for opponents, especially early in a match. Listen out for them and wait for them to come to you!

If you stand in a corner of a room there's only one place you need to aim your weapon - at the door. But your opponent doesn't know where you're going to be, which gives you the advantage.

Above all, never get involved in a fight between two opponents!

A three-way fight is never a good idea - you don't want to focus on two opponents at once.

They'll be concentrating on each other and won't know you're there - so wait and watch what happens.

One of them has to win, and then you'll be up against a weakened opponent - who'll probably be busy picking up loot.

You'll also have an idea of how good they are, and how carefully you need to approach them!

Also, don't forget crouching!

Crouching doesn't just enable you to duck down behind things - it also means you can move around silently.

This can be vital to surprising your opponents!

And when crouching you can use healing items - so it can be a smart move when you're under fire and need to hide and heal in a hurry.

If someone's trying to shoot you at long range, it can be quicker to find cover you can crouch behind than something that'll cover you while standing up.

If you need to move though a building - especially in the endgame, when it's likely other players are around - walk while crouching to avoid being heard. The only thing to remember is that crouching is bad when you're actually in combat – you're a smaller target but it's much easier for your opponent to get a headshot.

Plus of course you move around more slowly, and that makes you much easier to hit.

Just have your finger on the jump button, ready to come out of your crouch and launch into combat.

And your top priority should always be to look after your health!

Never go rushing into combat when you're at low health, however good you think your position is. One lucky shot can take you out!

Always carry some kind of healing item, which means if you don't have one, search for one (as long as it's safe to do so) before you move on.

And if you're not at full health and shield, always be thinking of ways to get there.

It's surprising how few players use campfires, for instance. They're a quick and free way to get your health back up to 100.

Remember where campfires are located, because they can often save you using a medkit - and they can be a lifesaver if you get caught in the storm!

In the early storm phases the campfire heals quicker than the storm does damage - so if you can keep it stoked up (which requires wood), you can take a breather there before making your way out.

Campfires can only be used once before they need to be restocked with wood - but they're used so rarely, they'll usually be available.

Likewise, remember where slurp barrels can be found - they're noisy but they're a quick top-up!

CHAPTER 4

"Tyler, I see you've finally got a decent skin then," is the first thing Ellie says when she enters the group chat.

"To be fair, Ellie," says Sana, "you've been wearing that one for ages."

"It's my look."

"I'm just saying –"

"Whatever." says Ellie, "Anyway, we need to get on with this, I'm going to the cinema at three o'clock."

Alfie's come over, because we always work best in the same room.

We're not really using different tactics from usual, but we want to be together so we can see how everything works with the new map.

So here we are - this is our first official practice for Llamafest!

Weirdly, Dad is in the living room too.

"Are you waiting to watch snooker or something, Dad?" I ask.

"No, you're fine," he says.

I try to pretend he's not there.

Of course, when it comes to the tournament we don't know what path the Battle Bus will take, so there's a limit to how much you can plan.

That's what's cool about the game, it's slightly random and always different each time.

But we've got a few nominated locations and depending on where the bus is going, we'll choose one of them.

Of course the other thing that'll make it different is the other players.

We've talked a lot about how the other squads in the tournament might play - will it be like a normal match, where lots of people jump out straight away and get stuck into the action?

Or will everyone try to play it smart... and come up with the exact same strategy, and land in the same place?

We've talked about it, and argued about it, and come to the conclusion that we don't know.

"We should focus on our own strategy," says Ellie over the chat as we wait in the lobby, "not what everyone else is doing, because it's better to make a plan and stick to it than have a hundred different plans that depend on what other people do."

"She's right," says Dad. "The best players in any game make you react to their strategy."

"Who was that?" says Ellie – my mic has faintly picked up Dad's voice.

"Er... that was my dad."

"What did he say?"

"He said you were right."

"Good. He's a smart guy, your dad. Smarter than my dad."

We check the path of the Battle Bus and Ellie declares we'll test out Strategy Four.

"Right," says Ellie, "our priorities are shields, materials and short-range weapons. We shouldn't need to engage in long-range combat, but if anyone finds an assault rifle, give it to me and I'll keep watch while the rest of you search the – Alfie, what are you doing?"

"Strategy Four."

Alfie's bailed out and is heading for the southwest corner of the map.

"That's not Strategy Four. We need to be going here." Ellie snaps, placing a marker on the map.

"I thought that was Strategy One."

"No, it's – hang on, what are the rest of you doing?"

"I dropped out when I realised Alfie had dropped out," says Sana. "I thought I must have got it wrong."

"No, you had it – Tyler? Where are you?"

"This is ridiculous," says Ellie. "Well, I'm sticking to Strategy Four."

"Shouldn't we stay together?"

"Yes! But it's a bit late for that now."

I check the map - we're all going to completely different places.

"Maybe we should name the strategies after where we're going to land," I suggest, "instead of giving them random numbers."

So with everyone scattered across the island, it turns out not to be such great practice for the tournament after all.

We're all on our own, sneaking around, trying to avoid other squads.

I'm particularly worried for Alfie, who might have to break his "no weapons" rule if he's going to survive this.

"Alfie," says Ellie, "this could be a time to try doing that thing we talked about?"

"Sorry," says Alfie, "but I still think a car counts as a weapon if you're using it to run people over on purpose."

"You could use it to run people over by accident though."

Sana and I both find cars and use them to meet up and then head for the storm circle - we've agreed a rendezvous point. (Ellie insists on calling it a 'rendezvous point', and corrects anyone who calls it a 'meeting point'.)

Alfie manages to open a rift and flies much closer to the rendezvous point.

Ellie takes out a whole squad by using explosives, which cheers her up a bit.

Finally, with twenty players left, we all meet up again - and Alfie throws us medkits and shield potions, so we can all heal up.

"This has actually gone -" Ellie starts to say...

Then the building we're in gets hit by a rocket launcher.

"That didn't seem to go very well," says Dad.

"No," I say, gritting my teeth.

We've got a lot of work to do before we're ready for Llamafest...

Marking the map is very important when playing with a squad – and it's useful in solo mode too.

At least one member of the squad should mark where you intend to land – and it's best to do this in the lobby, rather than while the bus is in flight!

If you're going to split up, the others should mark their landing places too – check on the map where everyone is going. And put markers down when you move around, too – make sure you all know where you're headed!

This is especially useful when you're using vehicles to move around the map.

When you take a trip in real life, one person drives and one person reads the map (or programs the sat nav, or whatever).

In Fortnite, my squad does the same thing – one of

us focuses on driving, someone else looks at the map and puts a marker down.

And someone else smashes the window and sticks their gun out to fire at anyone we see along the way... which is not something we do when taking a trip in real life, but it's good in Fortnite!!

(Incidentally, this is a perfect time to heal up - so choose the teammate who needs least needs healing to be the driver. Unless they're really terrible at driving!)

I even put markers on the map if I'm playing a solo match - if I need to go to a specific place or speak to a specific NPC, I'll mark the spot. It's just quicker that way, and stops you from getting distracted.

I also use the markers when driving, because you move faster on roads - and that means you can't always go in a straight line, as I usually do when I'm on foot.

Having a marker to aim for really helps me judge if it's worth following the road, or if I should just cut across the rougher terrain and go direct.

We all have favourite places on the map, but good players explore the whole island.

Most places you'll end up visiting just because of how the storm moves around - but there are still odd little places you can easily miss, which can turn out to be great places.

Can you really call yourself a pro Fortniter if you don't know the whole map?

And if the storm closes around somewhere you don't know very well, you're immediately at a disadvantage!

When you're in a place you know well, you can quickly find the good hiding spots and the stashes of loot - and that could make a huge difference.

I advise going to places when they're quiet - either land in them when they're not near the path of the Battle Bus, or go through them when everyone else is running towards the storm circle.

It can be difficult getting to know a new location when it's just entered the game and everyone is going there - so land near it, tool up, and then go there after the initial fighting dies down.

Places look very different when you're not getting into fights every ten seconds - you just notice a lot more, and you can explore them properly.

If you get to know places when there's not much going on, you'll be much better prepared if the endgame happens there!

A good rule in Fortnite is: when you're out in the open, don't stop moving, but don't move around too much.

Standing still when you've got no cover is a great way to get picked off from long range.

Even a few little movements, from side to side and back and forth, will help stop this happening - especially if someone's lining up a headshot, which is almost impossible when the target is moving.

If you're picking up someone's dropped loot, keep running and jumping around while you do it in case someone's waiting and watching.

Also, you need to know if anyone's coming up behind you, so keep turning around.

It can be annoying to do this over and over again while you wait for something to happen - but when something does happen, you're more likely to see it if you're not facing the other way!

However, lots of players make the mistake of moving around too much.

They get bored and want to explore another area, or another building.

Don't just do this for the sake of doing something!

The more you move around, the more chance you have of running into opponents - especially if the storm is forcing them your way.

Exploring and searching an area is a good idea early on, but when the storm circle gets small, claim a good spot and stick to it!

I hate being forced into the open, especially in the endgame - I much prefer camping out in buildings.

But I've found bushes are very underrated hiding places!

Position yourself correctly - and crouch down, to make sure your head doesn't stick out - and you can see out while making yourself hard to spot.

Opponents rarely expect you to be hiding in a bush, and will often run right past!

When you do camp out in a building, choose your spot wisely.

Basements aren't good places to camp out – if your opponent works out that you're down there, they won't come down after you.

They'll just throw a grenade down and take you out that way.

Medium-sized rooms are best – small rooms push you too close to your opponent, in large rooms they'll see you from a long way off, making it harder to take them by surprise.

You want to be close enough to get a clear shot in before they know you're there, but far enough away that they're not immediately on top of you!

CHAPTER 5

"Yes," I tell Mum, "I know I said I'd stop after the next match but –"

"But you want to play another one," says Mum.

"That wasn't what I was going to say."

"But you do want to play another one, don't you."

Well... yeah.

You agreed to stop after this one!

"But I messed up, it only lasted two minutes."

"Well that's not my fault, is it?" Mum turns to Dad. "Can you back me up here?"

"Yes," says Dad without looking up from his phone.

"That's not backing me up."

"Sorry," he says, then turns to me. "Your mum's right, you did say that - so what went wrong?"

"Landed in the same spot as someone else and they melee'd me to death."

"What's a melee?"

"When you hit someone with your harvesting tool."

"What's a harvesting tool?"

"Why do you keep asking me this stuff?"

"I told you, I'm just interested."

"It doesn't matter what went wrong," says Mum, "you've played enough for one day - you need to do your homework."

If Fortnite has taught me anything, it's that some battles aren't worth fighting, so I give up on this one.

But the reason I really wanted one more match is I'm so close to levelling up, and one more match would have done it!

Reluctantly, I go up to my room and get on with my homework – the last thing I want is to get banned from playing for getting bad grades, and miss the tournament.

While I'm working I set up a call with Alfie so we can talk.

(And I can ask him how to do stuff I don't understand because he's good at everything, school-wise. Even P.E. - he's surprisingly good at tennis.)

I'm moaning to him about having my session interrupted earlier, and how slowly I'm going up the levels. "You must play loads, you're much higher than me."

"Not that much."

"You don't even earn XP for eliminations, because you never make any - how do you do it?"

"I just focus on the quests."

"Does that make a difference?"

"Dude, it makes a huge difference!"

"I sort of do the quests when they pop up in the corner of the screen," I say, "but I don't really keep track of them. Why?"

"OK – you do your maths homework, and I'll tell you everything you need to know about quests."

So this is what I learned from talking to Alfie.

Playing the game normally doesn't earn you that much XP - you get bonuses for eliminations, surviving storm phases, opening chests and so on.

But they're pretty small, and even a Victory Royale doesn't boost it that much.

The big XP is all in quests!

There are five categories of quest, and conveniently they use the same colour-coding system as items - Common, Uncommon, Rare, Epic and Legendary.

If you've never investigated this, the list of quests is on your map screen - you just have to tab left to bring it up.

The quests work in different ways, and often these don't have much to do with winning matches - it's like a different system of rewards.

Common and Uncommon quests change every day, and they're usually pretty easy.

They can be something as simple as landing at a

named location, or harvesting materials - which is practically free XP.

Basically it's a reward for playing every day, and for paying attention to the Quests tab!

You should always try to do the Uncommon quests whenever you play - check what they are when you log on, because it's easy to build them into your play.

After you complete an Uncommon quest, a Common quest will pop up to replace it. You don't get anything like as much XP for these, but they're worth doing if they're convenient.

A thing to remember about Common and Uncommon quests is they get assigned to players pretty much randomly - which means everyone gets different ones.

If you're playing with a squad, your quests may mean going to different places and doing different things, so you'll have to agree who gets to do theirs first!

Rare quests build up throughout a season.

Typical Rare quests mean you have to eliminate a certain number of players, or travel a certain distance while swimming, or deal damage with a certain weapon.

Early in a new season, these are often really easy - the number you have to hit to complete the first one will be pretty low, like you might have to travel 1,000m while gliding.

Many of these quests can be completed without even trying - you'll end up doing them anyway.

As you keep playing, new versions of the same quest will appear - so next you might have to travel 2,500m, then 10,000m, then 25,000m and finally 50,000m.

You'll notice the gaps between those numbers keep getting bigger, so the quests keep getting more challenging.

This is turning into another round of maths homework...

Remember – even when these quests are complete, the game keeps tracking your progress, and the counter doesn't get set back to zero.

So once you've travelled 1,000m while gliding, you only have to do another 1,500m to hit the next target, if you see what I mean.

But the quests tab doesn't show your progress all the time – the quest only pops up again when you get closer.

This means that even when a rare quest seems like it's gone away, you can keep working towards the next one!

It's hard to hit the final target on these quests before the end of the season, unless you play a lot, so it's very likely you'll always have another target to aim for, even if you can't see it.

Make a note of the rare quests as they come up and what your last target was.

Otherwise, if you never get close to the next target, they might not pop up again and you might forget they were there!

Especially when they're something a bit weird, like melee eliminations. (Who does those unless they've just landed and haven't found a weapon yet?)

So keep a note and then you can keep working towards them, even when they're not on your screen.

Epic quests are a bit different, and often involve stuff that's specific to that season - going to certain places, talking to certain characters, and searching for things.

You sometimes need to do a bit of exploring to complete these, and knowing the map well is a definite advantage.

These quests will often give you big rewards - but they also tend to be things you won't complete just by playing the game normally.

Instead they're like side quests in an RPG, and they can easily distract you from the actual match!

It's always best to do them in the early stages of a match, in an area that's likely to be empty of other players, where you can work with a low risk of getting attacked.

All players get the same Epic quests - and many of them unlock at a particular point in the season.

When a new quest unlocks, lots of players will be trying to complete it - so if it's tied to a particular location, that location will be very busy!

This isn't the best time to do it - wait a couple of days. The quest will still be there - focus on some other quests instead.

In fact, this is a perfect time to go somewhere else!

If there's a spot that's usually busy, now might be your chance to explore it while everyone's away doing the quest.

Finally there's Legendary quests.

There's usually one of these each week, with a number of stages to it.

Often they'll work like Rare quests, like doing damage with a certain weapon, or they'll involve collecting a special limited item.

You only have a week to complete each one - but if you play in a squad, trio or duo with friends, you can work on them together, which is obviously much quicker.

So if you can get a bunch of XP-hungry mates together - especially if some of them are really cracked Fortnite players - you should be able to get through some Legendary quests!

CHAPTER 6

Thanks to Alfie's advice, I'm zooming up the levels.

But the downside is, this means even more things to explain to Dad.

"Why are you going over there?"

"I'm doing a quest. I have to drive a car from here to there."

"Why?"

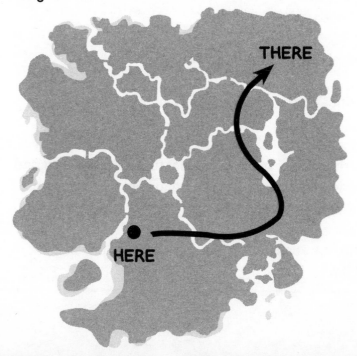

"Because that's the quest."

"But why is that the quest? I don't understand."

"It's just a thing you have to do, it doesn't really matter what it is, you just have to –

Then a hail of gunfire comes out of nowhere!

Before I even get to the car, I'm eliminated.

"What happened there?"

"I got into a stupid fight with an NPC."

"What's an NPC?"

"Non-Player Character, Dad."

"What's a Non-Player Character?"

I turn to him. "It's a character who isn't really involved in the match, but is there just to get in your way and generally be annoying by behaving in a completely predictable way, Dad."

"Oh," he says, not taking the hint. "We just called them baddies."

"What?"

"Back when I was a kid playing computer games. We'd just say 'Look out - baddies!'"

I sigh. "They're not necessarily 'baddies' - they're just characters who aren't controlled by players. Sometimes they can help you - though in Fortnite, if you fight them they will fight you back."

"Ah, I see."

I've got to say something.

"Dad... I'm trying to prepare for a tournament, and -"

"Oh, really? What's that then?"

"Llamafest, it's kind of a big deal - and it's just really distracting when you keep asking me questions."

"Sorry - I'll stop talking. You won't even know I'm here."

"That's the problem though, I do know you're here. ust knowing you're watching puts me off."

"Why?"

"It just does, alright? So can you not sit in here when I'm playing?"

"OK, OK." He slopes away to the study.

I feel a bit bad.

But this is important! There's not much I can do to make myself cooler in real life... but if I can improve my skills and get some good skins, I can be cool in Fortnite!

Maybe...

Anyway, NPCs in Fortnite - sometimes referred to as AIs - have taken lots of different forms.

Some seasons have had bosses and minions guarding loot strongholds, like Doctor Doom at Doom's Domain - or lone bosses who drop good weapons, like the Spire Assassins.

Others have had wandering groups of mercenaries, like the Marauders, who had a really annoying habit of blundering into an endgame situation and messing up your strategy.

Sometimes there are groups who pop up in predictable locations, like the IO Guards.

Then there's the more varied range of NPCs dotted around the island - characters with different functions, who you can buy items from. Some of them do other stuff too. You may also be able to hire or challenge them!

Knowing the locations of NPCs, and what they do, is extremely helpful in playing the game - sometimes it lets you know which areas you should go to, and which to avoid.

One thing to remember is NPCs operate the same way no matter what type of match you're playing - so an encounter that might be easy in a squad might be a real challenge in solos.

But here's the thing I find NPCs really useful for... any combat you get into with them usually counts towards damage and elimination-based quests!

This can be a great way to do quests that involve particular weapons, or that need you to do damage in a particular way.

Now, some NPCs are harder to fight than human players - but some of them are easier.

Some of them can take more damage than human players - but of course, if you're looking to notch up some damage, that can be good.

And the big difference between NPCs and human players is you know where they're going to be and you know what they're going to do.

Human opponents are unpredictable - some will be keen to fight you, some won't. Some will be great, some won't.

They might have any weapon in the game - they could be fresh from being rebooted with only a common pistol, or they could be packing a Mythic weapon.

They have an annoying habit of building forts to give themselves cover or a better vantage point.

And you can never find one when you want one!

NPCs can be approached early in a match, when you're fresh, and you can get that part of the quest done before things get serious.

Because you know where to find NPCs, you can prepare for the fight - get your shields up before you start! - and plan your strategy around the type of damage you need to do.

Maybe you need to make pistol headshots, which means getting in close.

Or maybe you need to make eliminations from long range - some types of NPC are great for this, as they wander around in the open and don't attack until you get close (or you attack them).

NPCs also fight in the same way every time, so if you've fought them before you'll know what to expect - and they're not as accurate as most human players, so combat is usually less frantic.

This all depends on the NPC, of course - some of them are really tricky! Zone in on the easier ones, the ones who don't move too much and give you a bit more time to aim.

This is particularly good when a quest requires you to make headshots.

You can usually find a few moments to line it up which you don't usually get with human players, who might crouch or jump-shoot at the crucial moment.

There's also wildlife.

Whether you want to kill animals is up to you – Alfie also refuses to do this, and Sana will only kill them if they attack her first.

But bear in mind that damage-based quests can also usually be completed by attacking wildlife, too!

Again, wildlife behaves more predictably than human players, and as an extra bonus, animals don't use guns.

This means they have to get up close to do damage, so if you're a good shot, you should be able to get them before they get you.

Avoid wildlife when you get to the endgame – they'll just do unnecessary damage and draw attention to you.

They'll usually appear in open areas, and if you don't want to fight them, the best way to get away is by building.

If you've got any food on you at this point, you can throw it to distract the wildlife - or even try to lead it towards your opponent by throwing the food in their general direction, though this would be tricky to pull off!

You can also tame animals, but it's tricky - you have to feed them and then tame them while they're distracted - and it's best done early in a match.

Finally, there's fishing.

This is something I never really tried until it popped up on the XP quests, because who wants to stand around casting a line into the water, making yourself a perfect target for opponents?

But it can be worth it!

Fishing spots are the best places to go - they're easily identifiable by the circular ripples of water.

And there are plenty of spots at the edges of the island which are unlikely to have anyone around... unless they're looking to use a fishing spot.

If you're concerned about being out in the open, just build yourself some cover. Make a little fishing shack. Perfect.

Fishing spots sometimes give you more than fish - you can also find materials, weapons and ammo.

Amazing what people just dump in the river these days, really...

If there's anything you're short of - for instance, you might be out of ammo for a weapon, without any chests or ammo crates nearby - fishing can be a lifesaver.

CHAPTER 7

No-one else says anything for a moment.

Sana and I are waiting to see how Ellie reacts, because the thing about Ellie is, she always needs to win.

"Explain that, please," says Ellie calmly.

We can't see her face - we're about to do a private session to make our final plans, and are talking over voice chat - but I think we can all imagine her expression.

"Well," says Alfie, "the top four squads in each round of Llamafest go through, right?"

"Right," says Sana.

"So all we have to do is survive, don't we? I mean we don't even have to eliminate anyone, we can let everyone else do it for us."

"No-one's going to take us seriously if we get through to the final without eliminating anyone," says Ellie.

"Do people have to take us seriously?" I say. "Will anyone even notice if we don't eliminate anyone?"

"I'm streaming this match for my YouTube channel so yeah, they'll notice. I want to win by playing well."

"We can go for it when we get to the final," says Alfie, "I just think we need to play it safe and make sure we get there."

"But what if we get a chance to knock out one of the best squads, so they don't get to the final?"

"How are we going to know who the good squads are, though?" says Sana.

"She's right," I add, "in the middle of a match we're not going to know who's who. We'll just have to decide based on whether we need to fight them, or if they're easy to pick off."

Ellie doesn't like this.

"What if everyone else tries to play smart and sneaky, though? Won't we all just be creeping around trying not to run into each other?" she says.

"Then we might have to change our tactics," says Sana. "But at first, we should be careful – and stick together."

"But what about if we're all tiptoeing around and we lose some members?" I say.

"That's a good point," says Alfie. "Usually you'd try to keep everyone alive so you'd have the best chance in the endgame - but we don't need to win in the endgame, we only have to get there."

"More chance of getting to the endgame if we're all alive," says Ellie.

"But let's not take too many risks. If there's a good chance you'll get eliminated trying to revive someone or grab their reboot card, don't. Just try to make it to the endgame."

"No, I don't agree."

"Ellie," says Alfie, "I'm not saying we shouldn't try to reboot each other -"

"You'd like it if I got eliminated early, wouldn't you?" says Ellie. "You're always complaining I attract too much attention."

"I'm not! I never complain about that."

"Not to me, but you complain to him." Ellie points at me.

"No I don't!" says Alfie, then turns to me. "Do I?"

I hesitate just long enough before saying "No, never" to make it obvious I'm lying. (I have warned Alfie how bad I am at lying, so this is his fault.)

Ellie has left the group call.

"That went well," says Sana.

Playing a tournament does seem to be raising the stress levels higher than normal, but... that's part of the excitement, right?

Talking of that... have you ever wanted to set up a Fortnite tournament of your own - like a full match, not just a Battle Labs session?

Well, not everyone can - your account needs to be entitled to run private matches.

This entitlement used to be really hard to get, and only big streamers and communities were allowed.

But now you can contact Epic Games directly for permission! It's not automatic - they decide who gets approved.

The first thing to do is set up 2FA - two-factor authentication.

This just means your account is better protected, with two steps needed to sign in. You can find this on the Password & Security tab in your account settings - just follow the instructions.

Don't forget that Epic staff will NEVER ask for your login details – these are stored securely and no-one needs to know them but you.

So if anyone asks for your password, they're scamming you!

The next thing is to send an email to:

tournamentrequests@epicgames.com

You'll need to explain what your tournament will be like and why you want to do it. (Be polite!)

If it's approved, you're good to go!

The main requirement is that you all need to be playing in the same region - so make sure all players know their matchmaking region should be set to the same as the host.

You can find this option on the Game tab of your settings.

Select the game mode you want, and click the custom match button on the game mode screen.

Now you can set up a password for your private match.

It's a good idea to choose it before you set up the match, so you can send it to everyone who's going to play.

All players need is the password - when they try to enter a match, this will tell the system to look for players using the same password and match them with each other.

So you'll need to send them the password via email or some other messaging system.

When you send the message, tell them all what time the match will start, so they can all be ready in the lobby - you don't want to be hanging around waiting for people to join.

(Oh, and tell them to make sure they've checked for updates earlier in the day...)

Make sure the password you're going to use is a valid one before you send it to everyone!

The password has to be between four and sixteen characters, and should only be made up of letters and numbers.

The game won't like it if you try to use something really obvious like "Password" or "1234", and may tell you to choose another.

Don't use the same password more than once - use a different one for each match.

So I might use TylersTourno1 for my first match, then TylersTourno2 for my second and so on.

But that might be too easy to guess!

You don't want randoms breaking into your match - so be imaginative and change up your password.

And if you're streaming your match, make sure your password isn't visible, otherwise everyone will be able to use it!

Players joining the match need to first make sure they're on the same region as the host, and then party up (unless it's a Solo match).

Then go to the Custom Match option and enter the password - if you're on a squad, the party leader will do this.

The host will be able to see the numbers go up as players join the queue. Once the match is full, it'll start - or you can choose to start it whenever you like.

If you're hosting, be clear with your instructions and make sure everyone knows how to join the match - don't leave half your players hanging around while you explain to the other half what they're doing wrong!

Hosting a match is like hosting a party - make sure your guests are happy!

Keep track of what's happening in your match - if you're eliminated, spectate the rest of the action.

If anyone has any issues with other players, you might want to see what happened - you can't kick people from a private match, but you can decide not to invite them to the next one.

Making a recording is a very good idea, especially if you're running a tournament with more than one round - that way you can check what order everyone got eliminated in, and who finished top.

I'm hoping the Llamafest organisers know what they're doing...

CHAPTER 8

So it's the day of the first round of Llamafest...

And we're all in the same room, which is a relief.

Alfie has apologised to Ellie for moaning about him behind her back, and they've made up.

Ellie has even agreed to be a bit more cautious than usual.

Unfortunately, I haven't quite made it to level 50, but I have unlocked some decent gear.

It's annoying though – just a few more quests and I'll have made it, and I can use that cool skin Sana likes...

We're all in my living room, because we agreed we could communicate better if we were all physically together.

And Ellie said my house was best because I've got decent broadband and I don't have any brothers or sisters who'll get in our way.

I haven't told her that Dad's been getting in my way quite a lot recently – he's been worse than an annoying little brother or sister – I just hope he doesn't come in and watch.

This might be difficult as I need to ask him a favour...

"Can I borrow your laptop?" I ask him.

"What for?"

"Because it's the tournament today, and we've only got three devices to play on - we need one more."

"Sorry," says Dad, "I'm using mine."

"What for?"

"Work."

"But it's Saturday."

"Work's very busy at the moment," he mutters and heads up to his study.

I return to the living room and let everyone know what the problem is.

"What are we going to do?" says Ellie - she's the one who didn't bring her own console. "You said we could use his laptop!"

"I said he HAD a laptop, I didn't know if he'd let me use it."

"Don't stress out," Sana says, standing up. "We've got plenty of time - I'll go home and get my Switch."

"I can't play on a Switch," says Ellie. "I hate the triggers."

"You can use the laptop, I'll use the Switch - as long as Mum's not using it. She's been using it a lot lately..."

When Sana comes back with the Switch, we get into the lobby.

We party up.

We check we've got our best bling on.

We all go and use the toilet one last time - just in case. Then Ellie enters the password and we're IN.

I'm not sure what I was expecting, but it's weird how at first it just feels like a normal match.

I watch out for other players bailing out of the battle bus, trying to judge how many are dropping early and how many are hanging on to the end. It seems like they're dropping in the same way they usually do... but it's very hard to tell.

We pick our spot according to Ellie's battle plans, not too far from the edge of the map – it doesn't look like anyone else is going for it.

All good so far!

"Now," says Ellie as we fall through the air, "if you do nothing else in this match, DO NOT get caught in the storm! We are NOT going out like that, right?"

"Right," we all reply. It's true, that would be the most embarrassing thing.

We all get to work harvesting materials, except Ellie who keeps watch and makes sure the sound of us demolishing a building doesn't attract attention.

We land, we tool up, we get lucky with the storm circle - we're still inside on the first phase.

"I see someone," she says suddenly.

We all stop breaking stuff for a moment.

The rest of us glance at each other - we don't want a cracked squad running over here to take us on this early in the match.

"Nah," says Ellie after thinking about it for a moment. "Too far away and moving too fast. Can't get a clear shot. Not worth it."

We breathe a sigh of relief and get back to harvesting.

I'm keeping an eye on the number of players left - it's definitely going down slower than it would in a normal match.

People must be playing more carefully...

Also it's impossible to know how many complete squads have been eliminated - that could make all the difference to us!

I guess we can't think about it that way - we just have to place as high as we can and hope it's enough.

The storm forces us to move on.

Alfie's convinced he hears someone moving around in a derelict building, so Ellie lobs a grenade inside just to be sure.

The explosion dies down...

...and then there's silence.

"There's no-one there," I say.

"Don't be so jumpy, Alfie," says Ellie.

Just then, a car drives out of the house's garage - and straight at us!

I'm the last one to react, and the car clips me, knocking down most of my shields.

The others get out of the way - but strangely the car doesn't keep going.

Instead it reverses, probably hoping to finish me off - but I dash out of its path and up the ramp Alfie's already building.

This should enable us to escape...

But then the car starts driving up the ramp after us!

"What kind of dumb strategy is this?" asks Ellie.

Alfie keeps building and the car keeps following.

It drives more slowly up the ramp, and we're just about able to keep ahead of it – but I daren't turn around and fire at them in case they catch up and ram us!

Sana and Ellie aim upwards and concentrate their fire on the car.

"I'm going to make a bend," says Alfie. "Be ready to turn..."

And he lays down a floor and then another ramp at a 90-degree angle.

We run up the new ramp – and I risk stopping to look back at the car.

"It's worked!" I say. "They can't turn around – there's not enough space!"

Then one of them smashes the car window and starts shooting at me with an SMG.

They miss! Haha!

But they've shot the platform I'm standing on - it collapses...

"Argh!" says Alfie as we both fall...

Sana and Ellie are quick to change tactics - Sana bashes her harvesting tool into the bottom of the ramp, demolishing it.

The car falls as the ramp collapses -

And Ellie is ready with a grenade, which the car lands on top of a moment before it explodes!

She'll be very pleased with that - great content for her channel.

(I'm jealous - I've never been great with explosives, I've been stuck on a quest to deal damage with explosives for AGES.)

One member of the squad is eliminated by the explosion, another runs out of the car and Sana and Ellie knock them down...

That means two of them are still out there somewhere.

There's no sign of them... either they were never inside the car, or they got away while we weren't looking.

"Excuse me?" says Alfie, who's been knocked down by the fall. "I'm on like 38 health here, can someone heal me?"

The missing members of the other squad seem to have bailed - they're not waiting to take us out and they're not coming back for their teammates.

We've won this one - but we've suffered for it!

As well as Alfie getting knocked down, the fall was enough to eliminate me completely, and Sana and Ellie took some damage in the final fight.

Sana revives Alfie and grabs my reboot card while Ellie finishes off the knocked-down squad member.

We notice they all had skins with hoods or helmets – that must be their thing.

We heal up and dash for the nearest reboot van – we're just gonna have to hope no-one's waiting to take us out when we get there...

At least this was no-one's fault – Alfie's tactics seemed really good at the time, and no-one could have guessed our opponents would drive up the ramp!

Who WERE those guys...?

It can be really off-putting when someone else does a bizarre strategy.

Sometimes they're just trying something out for fun – maybe they're YouTubers trying to get views for doing something weird.

Or maybe they just don't know what they're doing!?

Either way, a weird strategy can work if it confuses the opponent - so don't let yourself get confused.

Work out what you need to do to stop them!

For instance, I've seen people building ridiculously high before - so you can simply take out their fort from the bottom and make them fall.

Learning where weaker players go can be useful, especially if you're looking to make some early-match eliminations to bump up your XP.

This isn't always predictable, but over time you can spot places where you often do well after landing.

It's often locations that used to be really popular -the more ambitious players will have moved on to new locations, but you might find some players stick with the old ones.

Load up quickly on landing and you can rack up some good elims!

How do you react if someone starts shooting at you, and you don't know where they're coming from?

It depends on the situation. If you're on the edge of the storm and it's moving, focus on getting out of there before you look around for them - that's more important!

If you're close to some cover, get behind it. If you're near a building, get inside it.

And if you're already inside a building, find something to duck behind.

That'll give you a few moments to gather your wits and look for your attacker - and maybe even heal up.

This is when foraged items can be useful - you can eat them very quickly, whereas you're unlikely to have enough time to use a shield potion or medkit in this situation.

If you're in the open, try to work out where your opponent is.

Use the compass at the top of the screen - you'll probably have seen the red dots that appear there when someone shoots a weapon.

RED DOTS

The more attention you can pay to this during a match, the better!

Otherwise you'll have to wait for them to shoot at you again if you want to find out where they're shooting from.

If you can't see the opponent, they might be shooting at you from long range – in which case definitely throw up some walls to stop them getting another shot in.

And don't stand still – if they're using a sniper rifle or bow, they're unlikely to hit a moving target.

But if they're firing at you from mid-to-long range, they may be using an assault rifle – which can be used to pick off someone who's moving.

In that case, finding some cover is pretty essential!

If the opponent is nearby, don't try to run – it's no good!

Almost every time I try to dodge a fight when I'm out in the open, I get chased down and shot down.

You don't have any choice but to turn and fight.

Choose the right weapon for the range and return their fire, moving around as you go – I like to move backwards while I find my aim.

Gain a height advantage if you can – and if you can't, move towards cover!

CHAPTER 9

Sana reboots me while Alfie builds some protective walls around the reboot van and Ellie complains about how noisy the vans are...

I'm back - and we need to move again, the storm's almost on us. We pile into a truck and head for the edge of the circle...

We find a farmhouse, one of Ellie's favourite locations - from the top there's a good view across the landscape.

"We're going there," she says and none of us argue - we stop the truck at the side of the road and run over there.

Then I remember, while running through a cornfield... I have a quest to consume foraged items at the moment - I'm only two away.

If I can finish that, I'll level up to 50 for sure!

The others run on towards the farmhouse - but it all seems quiet, so I stop to slash down some corn...

Then I hear gunfire.

It's coming from the farmhouse!

"Help me!" shouts Alfie.

But the others are already under attack too!

"There's two of them!" says Sana. "Alfie's down!"

"I'm coming!" I say.

"Why aren't you already here?!" says Ellie.

"It's too late," says Sana. "They got us all."

"And they're DANCING."

"Tyler, come and get us," says Ellie. "There's only two of them and they'll be weakened by the fight - you can take them."

"No, it's too risky," says Alfie. "He should just try to stay alive until the endgame."

Ellie sighs. "You're right, he can't take them. Go on then, Tyler."

I jump into a convenient truck and drive away before the squad in the farmhouse realises there's someone missing.

"That's too noisy!" says Sana.

"I'm just using it to get away – I'll dump it in a moment."

"Find somewhere to hide and stay there."

Everyone's spectating me now.

"You'd better get us into the final, Tyler," grumbles Ellie. "We'd have won that fight if it'd been four against two."

I don't like this – too much pressure!

I dive out of the truck as soon as I reach another building and dash inside.

"Wait!" says Ellie. "Make sure there's no-one in there already..."

I equip my shotgun, crouch and creep through the corridors.

"Go up – get the highest ground you can find," says Alfie.

I already know this, but I don't want to break my own concentration, so instead of snapping at Alfie I stay quiet.

There are currently 31 players left...

I find a bathroom upstairs, close the door, crouch on the toilet and point my shotgun at the door...

And wait.

"Have you reloaded?" asks Sana.

"Yes," I say, then hit the button just to make sure.

The number of remaining players goes down, down... 23, 20, 18...

Then there's noise downstairs.

"That's a whole squad coming your way," says Ellie.

"Break down the wall and bail out," says Alfie.

"That's what you'd do."

"It's his best chance!"

"He can take them by surprise!"

"QUIET!" I say. I'm banking on Ellie being right – maybe if they split up to search the building I can pick them off one by one.

Footsteps approach.

The door opens...

I fire my shotgun – but it hits the open door!

I totally got my angles wrong there.

I adjust my aim and shoot again, and again –

But there's two of them – very wisely, they're exploring the building in pairs, and I go down in a hail of SMG fire.

And our squad has placed...

#5.

"Noooooooo!" says Ellie.

And I recognise the name of the player who eliminated me...

AvengingAymee0_0

That's Amy.

Revenge for embarrassing her at school, I suppose - she's probably been looking forward to that!

"I said he should've jumped out of the window," says Alfie.

"Shut up," says Ellie.

"What happened to you at the farmhouse, Tyler?" says Sana. "Why weren't you with us?"

"In a way," I say, "It's lucky I wasn't, because at least I stayed alive long enough to -"

"What happened?" says Ellie.

"I... was picking up corn."

Everyone lets this sink in.

"Why," asks Ellie, "were you picking up CORN?"

"I thought it might be useful."

"You were doing one of your stupid XP quests, weren't you?"

"A bit," I reply.

Ellie doesn't believe in doing XP quests - she thinks it's fine for Alfie to do them, because of how he plays, but for serious players they're a waste of time.

Ellie shakes her head. "Get out, Tyler."

"But... this is my house."

"I think you should probably do what she says, mate," says Alfie.

So, I messed up.

I got my head too much into XP grinding, and that's how I've started playing the game all the time.

I can't believe I let myself get distracted by corn - of all things! And now the whole squad - and Sana - is never going to want me to play on their team again.

I glance over at Sana but she has her head down and is busy stowing her Switch into her bag.

So I turn off the console, stand up and head for the front door - and I almost bump into Alfie's mum on the doorstep.

Obviously , the middle of a tournament match wasn't the best time to be thinking about my XP quests!

But playing with other people is really helpful to boosting XP - as well as the Legendary quests, where you can directly assist each other, there are rewards for reviving and rebooting.

You can also swap equipment if one of you needs to complete quests with particular weapons.

You can play matches where you don't expect to win at all, and just focus on XP grinding.

Or you can concentrate on that stuff early in the match - land in a place that suits whatever quests you want to do - and then after two of three storm rounds, ignore it and go for the victory.

Boosting your XP is really satisfying - but XP grinding can become, well, a grind.

Leave room to focus on the game! An endgame situation is always more exciting than, say, harvesting huge amounts of wood.

You don't need to complete every single quest that pops up to get to level 100.

If you're a regular player, there's more than enough time to get there before the end of a season.

Yeah, it's good to get there as quick as you can - but the quests that get you the most XP for the least effort, and the ones that fit naturally with your playing style, will add up to a lot of XP.

The daily Uncommon quests are usually quite easy, and can be completed in a couple of matches.

The amount of XP you get for each quest varies from season to season - but just doing regular Uncommon quests, and the early stages of the weekly Legendary quests, should get you there!

CHAPTER 10

No-one's talking to me - not even Sana.

I guess I deserve it.

After everything I said about playing carefully and focusing on the goal, I was the one who got distracted.

So much for being cool in Fortnite!

I'm hiding from everyone now - nothing to do except sit in a darkened room and keep grinding XP.

I'm trying to get some headshots, so I keep landing in busy locations and seeking out other players... and then dying within a couple of minutes and starting another match.

I wonder if a headshot on a chicken still counts as a headshot...

"So!" says Dad suddenly, clapping his hands – I didn't even realise he was there, and it makes me jump.

"What is it?" I say.

"How did your tournament go?"

"Rubbish."

"Oh?"

"I messed up and we missed out on the final by one place."

"Oh no. Still, you came close."

"Yeah, tell that to my friends."

"Do you actually mean that?"

"No, please don't tell my friends anything."

Dad watches me play for a few minutes, as I run into another player hiding in a basement. I'm on my assault rifle and try to switch to my shotgun...

But I haven't organised my inventory properly and I end up throwing a banana at my opponent.

"Is that what you're supposed to do?" Dad asks.

"No!"

"Then why are you doing it?"

The opponent eliminates me before I can even get a shot away, and I throw the controller down.

"I was actually going to ask if you wanted to play a match with me," says Dad.

I look up. "You?"

"Yeah."

"Me and you play a match together?"

"Yeah."

"Of Fortnite?"

"I thought it might be fun," he says as he turns and leaves. "Never mind."

On Monday morning I arrive at school, thinking how I can avoid my friends for the rest of the day.

As well as Sana and Ellie, there's also Leon, who's bound to have been watching and will know all the details of my failure.

I can't believe I'd forgotten about Leon...

I've completely under-estimated the potential for humiliation!

I can see them in the playground - it'd be great if I could just build a ramp and bridge over them and then smash my way into school through the roof...

But I can't do that, obviously.

I'm going to have to face them, by which I mean walk past them without making eye contact and hoping they don't speak to me.

"Why haven't you been answering your messages?" asks Sana.

"Dunno," I reply – but the real reason is I've turned off all my notifications and avoided looking at my phone as much as possible.

"We're in the final," says Ellie.

She doesn't look delighted by it.

"What? How?"

"Two other squads got disqualified for teaming."

(Teaming is when players who aren't on the same squad work together to eliminate other players.)

"I knew someone would try something like that to get into the top four!" I really did, I said to Alfie we should look out for it.

"Yeah yeah," says Ellie, "you're super smart. Anyway the rules say we have to stick with the same team, so we can't replace you."

"She wanted to replace you," says Sana, "I didn't and neither did Alfie. We all make mistakes, don't we, Ellie?"

I'm glad to know she's got my back on this!

"So how did they get found out?" I ask.

"Dunno," says Ellie. "I checked my video of it and didn't see anything. I tell you what I did find out though – the two who ambushed us in the farmhouse were from the same squad as the ones who drove up your ramp!"

"Did they make the final?"

"Yeah, and if I see a player in a hood called SecondToughest96, he's dead meat. He's the one who took me out. And then he did the default dance..."

I'm on my way to the classroom when I see Amy hanging around outside.

I walk over - she'll probably want to gloat a bit about how she eliminated me from Llamafest.

Well, that's OK if it means she's not angry with me any more.

"What?"

"You're welcome," she says, smirking and raising an eyebrow.

"What do you mean?"

"You're in the final because of me."

Wait - YOU reported those other squads for teaming?

Shh! Don't tell everyone.

I get it - Amy doesn't normally snitch on people, it's not her style.

Even if someone beat her by cheating, she wouldn't snitch - she'd get her revenge some other way.

So... why do it this time?

"If it hadn't been for you," says Amy in a low voice, "I'd have got into a fight with those boys last week and I wouldn't have been able to do the tournament at all."

Woah.

"I thought you were angry about that," I say, confused.

"Yeah I was at the time, but I thought about it and... actually it was good, and... you were sort of... being a good friend by doing it."

"OK, er... you could have just said that."

"Well I'm saying it now, alright?" snaps Amy. "Anyway when I realised you'd missed out because of those teaming losers, it seemed a good way to pay you back."

So Amy was not only grateful for what I did... she actually wanted to return the favour!

"Wow, thanks."

"Yeah alright Meeks, don't go on about it. Anyway, sort yourself out before the final, I took you out too easily in the first round. Learn some new tricks, eh?"

And she walks into the classroom.

I'm so surprised by everything that's happened, I almost forget to walk in myself.

It's easy to get stuck in your ways playing Fortnite, using the same weapons and ignoring certain aspects of the game.

And I've said before that if you've got a style of play that works for you, there's nothing wrong in sticking with it!

But from time to time it's worth trying things you haven't tried for a while - as well as anything new that comes in.

XP quests are great for helping you do this!

Often XP quests will be based around some new element of the game that's been introduced for a new season - basically it's a reward for trying it out.

If you don't like the new thing, well, at least you've earned some XP.

But you might discover something that's brilliant and well worth building into your game!

I have to craft an explosive chicken... ?

Similarly, quests will appear that involve things you already know you don't like doing.

Sana, for instance, hates using SMGs, and as I said, I'm rubbish with explosives.

Doing a quest based around something like this sometimes changes your mind – weapons are always being tweaked, and as you get more experienced at playing the game, you might find you've developed skills that help you use them better.

But it can also just be a huge pain in the neck.

Trying to fight with a weapon you're no good at using can really interfere with your game - it can get you eliminated.

So what can you do?

Of course, you can just skip those quests... or you can seek out easier targets.

As I've already said, quests are best done in the early storm phases.

This especially goes for quests that need you to fight in a particular way - the players you encounter towards the end are likely to be better, so you'll need your best skills to take them on!

Don't take a weapon you hate into the endgame just because there's a quest based around it. And remember what I said about NPCs - they're often good for tackling with an unfamiliar weapon, especially if they're the really dumb ones who only land one shot out of every five!

You can also make it easier by playing Squads.

Not because your teammates can do it for you - unless it's a Legendary quest, they can't - but you CAN make quicker progress on damage-based quests in this mode.

In Solo mode, opponents are eliminated immediately when their health reaches zero - but when playing Squads you can do further damage when an opponent is knocked down.

This is the perfect way to deal damage with weapons you don't like using!

Knock them down with the weapon you prefer, then switch to the other one to finish the job, when your opponent can't fight back.

You can also make headshots on a downed opponent and these can count towards any tally you are working towards on a quest.

Oh, and always look out for quests you can work towards in the lobby.

Usually stuff you do in the lobby doesn't count towards the real game - damage to other players certainly doesn't.

But sometimes you'll find actions like harvesting items, destroying structures or swimming, will count towards your quests.

Keep an eye on the totals in your Rare quests tab and see if they go up after you've done something in the lobby!

CHAPTER 11

A few days later, we're all back in my living room, ready for the final.

Ellie's talking a lot about how this has really pushed up her subscriber numbers, and lots of people will be watching us live and we need to make a good show.

I realise she's talking a lot because she's anxious.

I keep thinking I don't care what happens, as long as it's not my fault.

I know that's not the right way to think, but I can't help it - I just really don't want it to be my fault!

We've added something new to our strategy - in fact I can't believe we didn't think of it sooner.

It was Alfie's idea - he's got very into hiring NPCs when he plays Solo matches, unsurprisingly. It means he's got someone to do the fighting for him!

Ellie has pointed out to him that paying someone else to shoot people for you isn't really any better than doing it yourself, and I agree with her... but that's not important right now.

In the final, we can avoid getting outnumbered again by hiring an NPC to fight with us!

We've reworked our strategy to fit with this, because we need to land in a place with an NPC and make sure we hire them before anyone else does.

Sana's pointed out this could go wrong: the Battle Bus might not go near any of those places, forcing us to either abandon the idea or glide a long way to get there.

Ellie's argued we really shouldn't mess about when it comes to landing – it's more important to get on the ground quickly and tool up.

The more time we have to search the area where we land, the better kit we'll have when we leave.

But we all agree it's worth trying.

We get into the lobby early, figuring we want time to look at the map – we don't want to be the last ones in.

"YES!" says Alfie when he checks out the path of the Battle Bus – the end of the route goes right over a location that works for us.

We agree Alfie will do the hiring, because he's got plenty of gold – but he's got to wait until we've got the NPC to upgrade our weapons.

I'm feeling pretty good - I've got my Level 50 skin on and I'm totally focused on this match.

I just wish someone in the lobby wouldn't keep hitting me in the head with a harvesting tool when I'm trying to drop a pin in just the right place on the map...

"Is that Leon?" asks Sana.

It is. Of course it is.

Leon's squad was in a different match from us in the first round - I'd hoped maybe they were one of the ones that got disqualified for teaming.

But no - they won their match, and made more eliminations than any other squad in the competition.

Ellie moaned that he was "probably hacking", but that's what she always says about anyone who beats her at Fortnite.

She's spent a lot of time watching the video of Leon's match that he posted on YouTube, searching for clues on how his squad plays and how we can tackle them.

(She was also looking for evidence he was hacking, but didn't find any.)

"Don't let him get inside your head," I tell her.

"I'm not letting him get inside my head," she mutters. "He just really, really, really annoys me."

Anyway, she learned from watching him that his squad will probably bail out near the start but head away from the route of the Battle Bus. Based on this information we're unlikely to meet him until the end, if we meet him at all.

When it's time for us to bail out, we go on Ellie's count of three - and shoot towards the pin!

It's an area we've gone to a lot in our Squads matches, we all know where we're going to land - in pairs, Ellie with Alfie, Sana with me.

We even know where all the chests are and who'll take each one - as I drop, I'm already going over the route in my head.

It's all worked out...

"Uh-oh," says Sana.

"What?"

"Someone else is going for our landing spot!"

"Change course," says Alfie. "Land somewhere else."

"No!" says Ellie. "Alfie, get down there and make the hire - we can't afford to wait and upgrade our weapons, we'll just have to take what we get."

"I'm still not sure -"

"Trust me - stick with the strategy. This is how we win."

We stay on course...

And the other team veer off!

"Ha!" says Ellie. "They're scared of us."

She's right - they've panicked and changed their strategy, and they're trying to head for a different location.

"Watch them, Tyler," says Ellie. "See where they go."

I land and stand at the edge of the rooftop...

The other squad is landing on a nearby road.

"They're heading for that petrol station over there," I say.

"Ha! Perfect," says Ellie. "Put a pin on it."

I do it – and a moment later I hear Sana and Ellie firing assault rifles.

Wow, they found those quickly!

"Aim for the pump on the left," says Ellie. "Grab yourself a weapon, Tyler."

There's not a lot to choose from up here - Ellie and Sana have already grabbed the best weapons - but something's better than nothing, so I pick up a common shotgun.

Meanwhile the other squad are searching chests at the petrol station, and I wonder if they've realised what's going to happen...

The petrol pump we've been shooting at catches fire...

And explodes!

The other squad is too busy backing away from the explosion to pay attention to what we're doing - and as they're already damaged by fire, Sana and Ellie easily eliminate a couple of them from long range.

The others run away, and Ellie wonders whether to chase after them, finish them off.

"We should tool up here first, shouldn't we?" says Sana.

"Yeah," says Alfie, "they might be easy enough to deal with, but we could run into another squad on the way."

Ellie accepts this is a good point, but she's worried they might reboot their teammates and undo all our good work.

"We can see they haven't picked up the reboot cards yet," I point out, "so why don't you stay here and watch them while the rest of us search the building?"

Ellie thinks about this for a second. "That's a really good idea. If they come back I'll take them out."

I'm surprised Ellie's so keen on my idea - she doesn't usually like my strategy ideas!

"We can put markers down for any good stuff we find," says Sana, "and you can get them on your way down."

This all sounds genuinely good! That's the thing about Fortnite - sometimes the best strategies come up when you're in the middle of a match, you can't always plan them.

Sana and I head down into the building, where Alfie is waiting with our new hire...

Alfie has plenty of gold - it carries through from one match to the next, and there are lots of ways to get gold in Fortnite:

You can find gold in chests
Eliminated players drop gold
You can earn it by completing bounties or quests from NPCs
You get it for surviving a bounty
Most beds and sofas have some gold underneath if you smash them
Cash registers and safes can be searched for gold

If you make a point of doing all these things while you play, you'll never be short of gold!

PILE O' GOLD

If you have gold, use it - you don't get anything for hoarding the stuff.

The only time I might hold back on spending my gold is if I really don't think I've got much chance of winning the match, and want to save it for another match.

Certain NPCs sell weapons, allow you to upgrade the weapons you've got, and will sell you other items too. Knowing who's where and what they do can be crucial - they change from season to season.

Always upgrade weapons if you can, especially if they're Common or Uncommon - it's pretty cheap to upgrade as far as Rare.

The best part is, you can also hire NPCs for your squad!

First of all, of course, this gives you a numbers advantage - it's especially good when you're playing Solos and everyone else is only using Solo tactics.

If you can keep out of sight while your hired NPC engages with an opponent - the opponent will often be so distracted, that they won't know you're there until it's too late.

You can't control NPCs, so they won't necessarily go along with whatever strategy you're trying to use.

They especially don't understand hiding, and tend to wander around opening and closing doors and generally making noise.

Most annoyingly, they have a habit of demolishing

whatever you're trying to hide behind – attracting attention and wrecking your cover at the same time!

But if you're camping out, NPCs can make useful decoys – other players will be drawn out of hiding to attack your hired NPC, and then you can join the action.

Don't let your NPC do all the fighting for you – they can't heal and won't last long out there on their own.

Mostly you should work together to take down opponents.

(Unless you're Alfie, who does leave them to do all the fighting for him.)

However, they can be very useful in holding off opponents while you hide and heal up. And if it's late in the game, and you're really low on health and don't have any healing items, it might be worth letting your NPC go out there and try to win the match for you!

Also, avoid getting caught in the storm when you've got an NPC with you – that's a good way to lose them!

Bounties can either be started by accepting them from NPCs, or by visiting Bounty Boards.

As with quests, Bounty Boards can be a distraction from the main part of the game - so they're often best done earlier in a match.

However they do help you by showing you the area where your opponent is - so if you're looking to make some elims in a match, starting a bounty will lead you to a potential victim!

I've had matches where a bounty board was right next to the fort I'd made for the endgame, and it was a great way to find out where my opponents were.

If someone else starts a bounty on you, it can be wise to find a good spot to camp out and wait to spring an ambush - if you know they're coming, you can be ready for them!

Crafting weapons used to be done at crafting tables, but the game was changed to allow players to do this anywhere - if they have the right stuff.

Crafting materials are harder to find than building materials, but you don't need much of them to craft weapons.

If you've got the stuff, always use it to craft a weapon!

One of the big advantages of crafting is you can sometimes combine elements of two weapons into one, and save space in your inventory.

No need to carry around grenades and a mechanical bow when you can craft them into a mechanical explosive bow!

We're heading through a valley and Ellie's not entirely happy about having an NPC along for the ride - I know she secretly thinks it's cheating. (It really isn't! It's part of the game!)

But she also really wants to do well in this tournament - and we may come across another team using the same tactic. Which means all we're doing is evening things up.

"I can't tell her what to do," says Alfie.

"No," says Ellie, "but she follows you because you hired her, so if you stay out of my way -"

"I see someone!" I say.

"Where?" says Sana.

They've just come over the top of a hill nearby. We're actually not in a good position - they're much higher than us - but I don't think they've seen us yet, because it's dark.

The quicker we can take them out, the better!

Without thinking, I line up a quick headshot with my assault rifle -

And with two hits, the first one's down!

I shift my aim to the next nearest - and with more headshots I take them down too.

I don't bother to eliminate them, even though I'm close to completing another Rare quest for dealing damage - we need to focus on eliminating the others.

The other squad are reacting now, fighting back - but they're too late. My teammates have joined in, and in moments the last two opponents are gone.

"Was that you, Tyler?" asks Ellie.

"Yeah."

"How?"

"I had to do a lot of headshots to complete an XP quest, so after a while it just became automatic to aim for -"

"OK, we can talk about it after the match." I can tell she's impressed though. She won't say it... but she is.

We grab loot from the eliminated squad - and Ellie tells me to keep watch for other players.

The squad dropped a LOT of materials, so Alfie's happy - he does what we usually do, dashing across the dropped loot and grabbing all the materials and ammo.

Then he leaves the rest of us to check out the weapons while he dumps the ammo he's collected, since he won't be using it.

We've practised doing this, and we're pretty good at it now!

Alfie drops the ammo into three piles - he knows what weapons we usually prefer to use, and if we need anything different we just tell him.

He seems to really enjoy being the squad's supplies manager.

We never argue over who'll take which weapon, we've played enough times now that we always know as soon as we see a weapon who it's for - arguing over weapons is a time-wasting distraction!

"Does anyone want these grenades?" I ask.

No-one does, and I've got a spare slot – I'm happy switching from SMG to assault rifle, and don't really need anything else – so I take them.

We grab our ammo and head off...

It's getting tense – we're in the fourth storm circle, and it's closing around open space, which is exactly what I was hoping wouldn't happen.

I much prefer some buildings, a bit of cover – and though Ellie says she doesn't care and is happy to fight anywhere, she's a master at targeting people from the rooftops, so I know she'd prefer that too.

"Agh!" shouts Sana suddenly. "I'm hit!"

Someone's shooting at us from down by the river!

In a few moments, Alfie's built us some cover and Sana uses it while she heals. Alfie keeps building, up and up...

But the other squad's doing the same, and someone on their squad is a master builder – maybe better than Alfie!

Ellie tries to get a sight of them, but can't – they're building too quickly, and keeping out of sight...

And they're using fire weapons! Our fort's on fire!

Alfie stays calm - he tells us all to bail out of the burning fort, and immediately starts making a new one from metal behind the old one.

This is a smart move - our opponents won't be able to see the new fort until the old one burns down, which means the longer build time of metal shouldn't be a problem.

I could just wait here... but that fort keeps getting higher and higher... and I've got an idea.

Their fort's at the bottom of a slope - which means a well-aimed grenade should come to rest at the bottom of it!

There's a tall bush up ahead, which I think I can reach without being seen... they're probably all watching the fire to see in case anyone comes out of it...

I dash over there. I line up a grenade...

And throw it!

There's no point waiting to see if it hits the target. I may as well throw a couple more while I've still got the element of surprise!

This is how I eventually completed those explosive eliminations quests that were annoying me so much...

The first grenade takes away the bottom layer of walls - the fort starts to collapse...

I toss another grenade over there - why not, this is the best moment to use them!

And the whole fort comes down!

Sana and Ellie start firing on whoever's left. I run from the bushes, SMG at the ready –

And get knocked down immediately.

The battle rages as I try to crawl back into the bush.

"Got who?" says Alfie.

"My nemesis!"

And yes, there it is on screen: El_Scorcho_999 shotgunned SecondToughest96. The hooded player who eliminated her last time.

And that's it, the whole squad's gone!

"Where are you, Tyler?" asks Sana.

"Knocked down, in a bush."

"What are you doing in a bush?" asks Ellie.

"Hiding. And dying."

Sana dashes over and revives me, but then there's gunfire coming from the other direction...

"Need some help here!" says Alfie.

Our fort's under attack from the other direction now – and Alfie and our NPC are the only ones defending it!

I stay inside the bush to heal while Sana and Ellie

run to defend the fort – and I realise there's only nine players left. We're nearly there!

There's just one player attacking our fort – is that the survivor from our first attack, right at the start of the match…?

I join the others at the fort to find the NPC has already eliminated him.

"Haha!" says Sana, recognising the username that flashes up. "That was Leon."

"That's shameful," laughs Ellie.

But we need to look out now. Where's the last squad? The storm circle's really tightening now…

There's a noise, over by the river!

A hovercraft left abandoned on the bank is moving across the ground towards us.

"That's a weird tactic," says Sana.

"Concentrate your fire," says Ellie. "Blow it up!"

We all fire on the hovercraft at once - it's not moving very fast but it's pointing our way, which means...

"Missiles!" I shout.

That's clearly the plan - it's going to fire off missiles. But those things are so hard to aim...

Unless you're an expert, and whoever's driving that thing seems to be an expert!

The missiles hit our fort as we bail out of it - but Alfie's not quick enough. He's gone!

"Don't revive him!" says Ellie, which sounds harsh but she's right - we need to deal with the immediate threat -

But there's another threat coming from behind us. The hovercraft was just a distraction!

Man, that's clever.

Ellie's managed to blow up the hovercraft, taking one of the other squad with it - but Sana and I are both shot down before we can even take aim.

I recognise the player standing over me as she aims her shotgun to finish me off at close range...

ELIMINATED BY AVENGINGAYMEEO_0

Amy. AGAIN!

That girl's good.

Ellie puts up a good fight, knocking down another member of the squad - but Amy eliminates her too.

It's over. We placed #2.

So close!

I look up, expecting Ellie to be furious. She puts down her controller, looks up at the rest of us...

Well I thought we were awesome.

And we all agree. We were awesome!

The longer a match goes on, the more adaptable you have to be - because your options close down as the storm closes in.

You'll be forced into areas you don't like to fight in and you'll have fewer chances to pick up weapons and items - in fact, the best way to get fresh loot in the endgame is to make eliminations.

OK, we can either go up the mountain, or we can go up a different mountain.

And of course, you can never predict where the storm will go! We've all come up with brilliant strategies that have got ruined when the storm circle moved to an annoying place.

This is where you can run into problems if your strategy is too heavily based on building.

Some players will stay inside their fort for ages and refuse to come out into the open: if an opponent shoots at their walls, they'll just keep repairing and rebuilding them.

This can be effective if you draw the opponent closer to your fort, then hit them when they're not expecting it – the moment they need to reload is often best for this.

But you HAVE to know what your exit strategy is if your fort gets caught in the storm!

Some players build sideways, making ramps and platforms to get themselves back to safety.

This is a good skill, if you can do it – but it can leave you very open to attack, especially if the storm has pushed you close to your opponents.

Can you do it under fire? If you're playing Squads, can you all stay organised enough to move quickly as a group?

What if your opponents break down the part of the fort that's holding you up, and you fall to the ground and you're a sitting target?

When it comes to the endgame, don't leave it too late to go into combat!

The longer you leave it, the more random things get.

You might get lucky and your fort will end up in the storm circle, forcing your opponents to move and giving you a chance to strike.

Or you might not!

Plus, when the storm circle forces you into super-close combat, things can get REALLY random!

It can be hard to aim when an opponent is so close, whereas a lucky shot from them can take you out immediately.

Of course, you might be the one to make the lucky shot - but we don't rely on luck, do we? We're pros!

It's always better to finish a match before it gets to that stage - so don't wait too long, and know when to go on the offensive.

If you're up against a player who's camping out in their fort, you can use explosives or flame-based weapons like I did - but if you don't have any, this is when your ammo supplies become essential.

Tackling fort campers can take a lot of ammo - so if you've got it, you're well set up.

I've always said the assault rifle is THE essential Fortnite weapon, because it combines effectiveness at range with a fairly quick rate of fire.

It's also great for battering an opponent's fort from medium range!

(If you're closer, switch to the SMG - its lack of precision isn't a problem when your target is a wall, and its rapid fire-rate will make short work of it.)

Either shoot away the foundations of the fort (which can be awkward - you won't always have a clear sight of them) or target the wall your opponents are hiding behind.

If you're in a squad, get everyone to concentrate their fire on one wall - together you can break it down faster than they can repair it.

You might get a split-second where you can do some damage before they get their wall up again – make the most of it!

It may come down to who runs out first. Will they run out of materials, or will you run out of ammo?

If you've been stocking up on ammo you won't have to worry about this – you can wear them down.

You've got them on the defensive, so try to keep them there – they're stuck repairing and rebuilding, and can't do much else.

At this point most Solo players will realise they need to change things up if they're going to win, and then they'll move.

Squad players might leave one player on repair duty while the others try to take you out – but you can quickly shift your fire to them.

It's all about forcing an opportunity to win – don't leave it too late!

CHAPTER 13

We're celebrating our silver-medal success - which earns us the runner-up prize of 2,000 V-bucks each! - with fizzy drinks and Nutella-and-marshmallow toasties, and I'm texting Amy to congratulate her on winning.

She replies with a gif of a dancing cartoon pig.

I AM DE BEST

You did OK too Meeks

A friend request pops up on my screen... from SecondToughest96.

"My nemesis!" says Ellie.

I decide to accept it – I'm curious to know who this is...

Immediately they invite me to a Squads match.

Alfie decides to sit this one out, but Ellie and Sana are keen to get involved – especially Ellie, who wants a win after all that excitement (I know the feeling).

We enter the lobby and I turn on the voice chat so we can hear this mystery player...

"Hello?" says SecondToughest96. "Is this thing on?"

Wait! I know that voice...

Alfie drops his toastie.

"HE'S my nemesis?" says Ellie.

"Since when do you play Fortnite?" I say.

"I thought it might be nice to know a bit about this thing you're all into, and I got talking to the other parents and they all had the same idea, and when Tyler told me about this tournament -"

"Wait..." says Sana. "Other parents?"

"Yeah - your mum, Alfie's mum and Ellie's dad."

"Oh no," says Sana. "I've been dreading Mum getting into Fortnite - she's so competitive. This is going to be unbearable."

"She's very good at building."

"Well yeah, she is an architect."

"And Alfie's mum is absolutely deadly with the Shadow Tracker."

"What?" says Alfie. "That doesn't make sense at all? She's the one who banned me from from playing violent games!"

"Hang on," says Ellie, "so this means you lot got through to the final of Llamafest?"

"Yes," says Dad. "In fact we finished fourth."

"So you must be... quite good?"

"I suppose we must."

Ellie looks quite impressed, but Alfie is still opening and closing his mouth.

After the match - which we win, by the way! - everyone heads off, keen to go back to their parents and check it's really true, and Dad's not just winding them up.

I go to the door to see Sana out, still talking about the game - because it's just easier to talk about the game than to talk about other stuff.

"I still don't really know what my role in the team is," I tell her. "Like, I don't know what I'm good at."

She smiles. "You do the stuff no-one else thinks of doing."

Then she leans over and kisses me on the cheek.

Later that evening, Dad and I sneak off to the living room after dinner to have a quick match. This could work out well for me after all.

THE END

DON'T MISS...

INDEPENDENT AND UNOFFICIAL

SECRETS OF A FORTNITE FAN

One fan's journey to Victory Royale!

A HILARIOUS ADVENTURE FILLED WITH FORTNITE TIPS!

EDDIE ROBSON   OSCAR HERRERO

TYLER'S FIRST FORTNITE ADVENTURE!

INDEPENDENT AND UNOFFICIAL

SECRETS OF A FORTNITE FAN

LAST SQUAD STANDING

ONE FAN'S ADVENTURE FILLED WITH FORTNITE TIPS!

EDDIE ROBSON

OSCAR HERRERO

THE ADVENTURE CONTINUES!